Storm City
Onyxsia Saga

By Solomon Abrams

I0556937

Storm City
Onyxsia Saga
By Solomon Abrams

Table of Contents

Storm City: Onyxsia Saga

Storm City

Onyxsia Saga

Solomon Abrams

Solomon Abrams LLC
Address Withheld
Chicago, Illinois, 60637
UNITED STATES OF AMERICA

ISBN:978-8-9893429-5-2

September 2024

Storm City: Onyxsia Saga

Sight & Sound

Saint sat against his parked Zephyrus X7 hoverbike, staring up at the darkening sky. The corporate radio feed had been predicting rain was coming, which was an easy thing to forecast. However Saint trusted his instincts; there was a storm brewing different from others. The wind smelled manufactured and sterile. As if it were being blown through an air conditioning unit. The way it smells on the larger off planet transports. That in and of itself was strange. Saint Seraphim inhaled deeply, processed the air in his lungs then slowly exhaled. The air was thick and heavy with cool moisture. His instincts told him to prepare for a storm, he had been a Dark Rider too long to disregard his instincts. Onxyisa was an island city, situated between two massive mountain ranges, the people called them the Goddess Hands, and two rivers that form a large delta that flows out to the ocean. There is always a storm of some kind pissing rain on the city. Add in monsoon season and any idiot can say there will be rain. But this report was a bit different. Corporate reports were predicting a larger than normal unseasonal storm that included high winds and *flooding*. Something about the reports didn't sit right. There were rumors moving through the citizens, speculating everything from this being the mega storm spoken about by the holy people to another plot by the Off-Worlders to completely break away and leave them here. Whether Apocalypse or Anarchy, it meant more business for him as a security courier. The elite loved their secrets. And secrets needed to be protected. Outside of rain, Onxysia had an abundance of secrets. Secrets they paid couriers like him a lot to safeguard and transport. Tapping the side of his visor, activating his helmet, Saint tossed his leg over the X-7, and started the whisper quiet hover bike then pulled up vertically into local air traffic. There were virgin runs to make before the rains came and the real courier jobs -Dark Jobs, started.

Another thing that Onxysia had in abundance was technology. The city used the technology to convert, store and harness the energy created by the weather phenomenons that occurred. The city was built on a series of dams and turbines, of varied sizes, used to fulfill the immense need for electricity. Each skyscraper was designed with a lighting rod system that not only saved the structure from destruction but acted as massive surge protectors and power reducers. The rods direct lighting surges into battery units and grounding stations. This allowed the city to collect power and export batteries of different sizes and uses throughout the planet and off world. Onxysia was the hub for electro-commerce. The region was the primary manufacturer of the power devices for spacecraft. There were even electricity harvesters who sold batteries and volt boxes on the underground market. They also built the intricate electrical circuitry and devices for weapons. Which is why Dark Riders like him were needed. The amount of corporate espionage that happened was staggering. It was its own industry with a different set of laws. And since most of the city and its people were connected via the internet, important information was transported on, external devices, or *bricks*. With all of this technology based on electricity and cybernetics, most elite or those rich citizens were enhanced with circular circuitry that ran over parts of the body. As the circuitry became more sophisticated and artistic it grew to be known as Cyber Veining; veins for short. These markings became popular. So popular that when people realized you could use the veins to receive and transmit information, secret communication styles were created. One very popular one was a pirate broadcasting network. How it works is, you find a place to connect to, exposed skin to circuitry and listen to the feed. There were larger gathering places known as cafes or campuses where people could jack in. This is how Saint got the information he could trust. This broadcast was what he was listening to when an order for a special delivery came through.

"We believe the Offworlders are using this impending rain to hide their movements." Lekeisha Shaw; the voice of the New Hive, said. Her voice was sultry and passionate. He, like many of the citizens in Onxysia, believed her. Something was amiss. But before Saint could put any real thought to the conspiracy a soft rhythmic melody cut into the feed. Saint triple clicked the small circuit splice just under the skin of his left hand. It was a biomechanical safety measure for couriers. I switched the feed to an encrypted secure line for short communications.

"Clean Line 60 seconds…" Saint whispered looking around the bustling cafeteria. He had stopped in after delivering a virgin package and waited inside away from the heavy rain. He lifted his jackets allowing his exposed back to connect directly against the wall.

"70,000 credits. Hostile level Orange; Extreme priority. To accept, go to the counter and order coffee black, almond milk on side."

Saint stood, severing the line and fixed his jacket. He walked directly to the counter and ordered. The waitress frowned slightly then offered, "this coffee should keep you warm and sharp."

Saint reached across the counter to pay, just as the waitress Diedra; her name tag read Diedra, was sliding the cup across to him. Their wrist touched for a second and the coordinates for the pickup and delivery were passed from her to him. Saint walked outside, took the top from the warm coffee and guzzled the contents. There was a small tracker capsule at the bottom that he swallowed and chased it with the smaller cup of warm almond milk. He hopped on his bike and moved quickly into the shadows and back streets.

The pickup was close. The person who handed him the small metal block was purposeful. They only spoke to give Saint the commands to verify him as the proper courier. An infrared light was shone in his face. They told the dark night shadows that Saint was clear, signaling that the sniper who watched over them didn't have to eliminate Saint. The Download was slow and deliberate, taking a few seconds longer than before at the cafeteria. This download was the actual delivery. The box was most likely a decoy. It held some information but mostly it could be discarded. Some people allowed the couriers to keep the decoys to be sold later, The real deliver was a secret someone needs to be downloaded directly to the receiver. It was information that would be downloaded directly to Saint and in turn Saint would download it directly to the receiver. Saint and the person connected their wrist and kissed; tongue to tongue. Then 15 second later Saint was back in transit. Part of the download was a map that played through the feed in his helmet visor. It showed him the exact route, including a back entrance where he could pull into. Saint moved through out the city's traffic, as if by memory. There was something very familiar about this route. The streets were busy with people doing their last minutes errands and shopping before settling in to wait out the storm. The gentle vibrations of the hover bike between his legs and the buzzing from the downloads caused a growing sexual excitement to course through Saint. Everything inside of him slowly became alive. His senses were heightened but in a way that made him want to be "experienced" intimately. He turned down the back alley, slipping into a small space. He didn't notice the door slide quietly behind him concealing the secret entrance he just used. He only noticed the pulsating from the head of his member and reverberating throughout his body. He walked down a green dimly hallway into what was a garage. There was another hoverbike parked beneath the cool blue light of the security drone. The bike was a custom built, speed hoverbike, barely legal. It was a Falcon Zx5. Saint knew the biker and the rider. Dr. Nashia Indine was a doctor of Hydro-Engineering & inventor by day and a street hover racer by night. As well as a frequent partner of Saint. They hadn't seen each other in months due to her off planet work and his schedule. Or that's the story Saint had told himself anyway. The thought of her touch and their last experience sent a deep tantric shudder through him. He missed her. He could feel her now. He turned down another hall, this one less clandestine and walked toward what he knew was a large warehouse space Nashia's team had been using as a laboratory. The hallway was dimly lit; every other light fixture was powered. At the end of the hallway was two large metal doors. Saint could hear the voices of two women, one he recognized as Nashia and the other he surprisingly recognized as Lekeisha Shaw. Just as Saint got closer, the doors slowly swung   open revealing the two women.

"and here he is now." Nashia said smiling. "Lekeisha Shaw this is Saint. He is the courier we spoke of"

Saint stood erotically dumbfounded and overwhelmed by a sudden rush of stimulation. Nashia seemed fuller and more inviting. It was as if she was larger than the last time he "saw" her. But her physical appearance wasn't the reason for his feeling. There was an ethereal sound and aural light coming from behind them. Saint smiled, not noticing his length growing and creating and large bulge. He extended his hand and smiled.

"It's nice to meet you Le-"

He was cut off by her beautiful smile and a waving hand. "Please call me Shaw." She took his hand and stealthily tapped his inner wrist, sending a slight jolt and download into him. Saint looked into her eyes, frozen for a second. "You were right, He is the perfect courier." She said over her shoulder then turned back to Saint. "Believe you have a package for me."

It took Saint another moment to realize she meant the box. He pulled it free and handed it to her. Shaw took the box and spoke to them both.

"I'll be on my way. This storm is upon us and we all have work to do." She nodded then moved down the short hall, only she left out of a different non descriptive door than Saint, who wasn't sure if the door was there when he walked past or not.

As Shaw disappeared, Nashia suddenly hugged Saint. Her embrace was deeply passionate and telling. She missed him too. "We have work to do and I know you have questions. However with time being of the essence I need you to trust me."

Saint nodded his head, acknowledging that she had his trust. "I need you to come into the lab and get undressed. Go into the locker room and shower then meet me in the lab. She turned and walked toward the laboratory. She pointed toward the room. "Hurry Saint! I'm tired of waiting on that dick."

Saint laughed as a small orgasm moved through him with a bit of ejaculated fluid.

Minutes later, freshly showered and rejuvenated Saint stepped into the laboratory to see a massive glowing structure. There were three large gyroscope style rings of different colors; pink, blue and white. The rings, one slightly larger than the other, orbited a large bed like platform. The rings hummed with three different tones. The tones sounded like voices to Saint. Each "voice" spoke to a different part of him. He was mesmerized. It took Nashia's voice to slightly bring him back. She was naked now and Saint could see her completely- she was bigger. Just slightly but it was noticeable. She smiled at him.

"As you can see I'm a bit different. Being off world changes you. You find out first hand." She stood in front of him, taking his hand in hers. Their bodies touched just slight "My love listen closely. I'm taking you away. The download you carry is roughly a millennia of knowledge. But to extract it we have to make love. It's quicker and more effective. You were chosen because I ; well WE, needed someone that could be trusted." She stared directly into his eyes. "Do you trust me?"

"I do." Saint answered.

"May I have your complete self to do as I need?"

"You May."

" Will you join me in life?"

"I WILL..."

He hadn't noticed she was stroking his member now.

"This is going to be amazing. Please go lay down on the platform while I get things ready. You'll see. Once things get going we won't be able to use words. Well not in the way you're used to."

She stepped back and grinned.

"So what is all of this?" He asked walking toward the platform. The space in the room was large but he acoustics allowed for them to sound clearly.

"Over the last few years I've been working to assist the Corporations with space travel. Specific the use of water and other fluids for energy use. During that time we stumbled onto sound and vibrations. We learned that if used properly vibrations could positively effect growth in biological systems and process. In short we used sound and water to grow things. As you can tell my body is more voluptuous and curvy. I've grown three inches. My breast are larger. Legs thicker. Even my ass is bigger." She turned and shook her butt for a second before laughing. "Even now just being in this room you've grown thicker and longer. Not much but enough that I noticed"

Saint looked down at his fully erect member. It didn't seem longer to him but it was girthier.

"So along with that, we learned that we could use sound to communicate across space, time and dimensions. We had a massive exchange of information. So much so that WE have created a Cosmic

University. What you're standing on is known as a sonosphere."

Saint watched her flick switches and turn knobs.

"They used it for a primitive form of healing." She hit a switch and the room became filled with sounds. The rain. An amplified aural humming and what felt like heart beats. "We used to for our agriculture task." She turned a knob and a few things happened at once. The room slowly grew dark, the only light being those of the things. The ceiling slowly became translucent giving them a clear view of the night rain. It was if the roof never existed. And lastly, the rings began to turn on their axis. By the Nashia had joined him on the bed. She crawled over him coming face to face with him. She lowered her voice with each word.

"I'm apart of the team that created this storm. It doesn't rain in space so we had to create rain here, to be collected and taken into space. However we believe the Corporations have a different plan and I, well WE need your help, Saint."

She was straddling him. He could feel her hands on his member. She was guiding him inside of her. She sat down on his length and a passionate moan rushed from her mouth. She turned his forearms over then pressed her forearms against his and started the download. Saint watched the rings of the gyro separate and increase in speed there was a harmonious whooshing, then a slight vibrating began engulfing them. Saint's being felt as if it was separating into different equal parts; mind, body, and soul. The sound of the rain, the whooshing and the humming grew. Nashia was right, he couldn't speak. He heard-felt her voice deep inside of him. In every part of him. Yet it was if she were singing to him. She moved her pelvis up and down in harmony with the whooshing. She felt, warm snug and inviting on him, around his girth. A warm wetness slowly began coating the area between their legs.

Saint embraced her, touching her body for the first time. She interlocked her fingers into his. Saint lifted his head and allowed her breast to fall into his mouth and began suckling her nipple. Nashia cursed and threw her head back.

The ethereal harmony of sonosphere was joined by the vibration of the rain drops. Saint opened his eyes and was overcome by the visual of the lights and Nashia. She looked angelic. As if she were an angel, her deep brown skin seemed purple, fuchsia then onyx as the lights changed colors.

A soft whisper engulfed Saint from all around and inside of him, "I missed you."

She whispered. "I need you." Her voice felt like he was swimming in her words and that they were floating. Nashia leaned forward and dug her teeth into his chest, then rolled them over positioning Saint on top. He reset himself for balance and comfort. Saint drove himself slowly and deeply into her, then let the cosmic current drive his movements. He lifted her legs up to his shoulders and began kissing her. They were engulfed in a cocoon of light, sound and vibration. It was overwhelming. He felt the raindrop vibrations on his skin but not the wetness. Saint's skin tingled and buzzed. The energy inside of the sonosphere was nearly suffocating. The orgasmic sensation of swimming swept over him. He peered up and saw different images. It was different versions of them. In one version his head was buried between her thighs. Her breast were large and her nipples pierced. They were laying on a blanket in a colorful forest. In another image they were younger, he was leaning against a wall, pants pushed down to his ankles. She was slowly taking him in her mouth. Saliva dripped from her greedy mouth. In another their genders were reversed. In another vision they were older. Everywhere Saint looked he saw different versions of them making love, passionately fucking or simply fooling around. Saint was near an explosion he looked down at Nashia, suddenly filled with information and understanding. He felt as if they were becoming one being.

"We are the HIVE." He felt her say.

"We are the HIVE" he repeated with his entire being. His hips moved and drove him further into her. He growled and panted. The energetic eruption was growing like a storm. He moved and stroked. She rolled her hips beneath him. They moved both in passionate unison as well as independently of each other. Saint felt his body succumbing to the waves that were passing through him. A warm fluid explosion started in his loins and flowed outward from his sexual epicenter. And suddenly he knew everything. He knew everything she knew and transferred his knowledge to her. She soon erupted coating them both in her fluids and passion. They rolled for moments more. Saint lost track of time, allowing Nashia to guide them. There was a full explosion of rainbow light and muffled sound. It felt as if he were falling down a tunnel of warmth and light through a prism. Suddenly things went black.

Saint softly opened his eyes and stared up at the ceiling of the lab. His body felt warm and rejuvenated but empty and clean. There was a throbbing in his head but no pain.

He turned his head to see Nashia laying naked smiling at him.

"What time is it?" He asked

"Thursday…" Nashia said laughing softly.

Saint sat up shocked. "I've been sleep for two days?"

"No my Love, it just seems like that. Time is different for us. You'll get used to it."

She stood revealing her beautiful nude body. Saint could see where he been sucking and biting on her delicate brown skin.

"Time to get dressed Lover. The storm has gotten worse and we have work to do before we leave."

"Where are we going?" He asked, slowly standing, he was a bit woozy and not weak.

"OffWorld. I'll explain as we go. As I said before, the Corporations have a plan and are using this storm to cover things up. They may actually break the city"

"Wait what.."

She pulled him close and kissed him.

"We have to go. Shower and get dressed. We have to go"

The Echos of Thunder

(*Days Before Storm*)

Isibo sat in his office overlooking looking the rear of the tenement and watched his neighbor Zuri. She was hanging what he believed to be small clear globes along the stone wall that acted as the rear border of the property. She was a small framed pretty light coffee brown woman. She was usually quiet, and soft spoken. She moved like a dancer; light and agile, almost if she were tip-toeing.

He had been cleaning his weapons when she caught his eyes. He had his window open enjoying the breeze and smell of the impending storm. The breeze felt good but the smell was off. It had an artificial scent to it. He had heard the rumblings throughout the city and he began preparing for what was to come. He would get out in the street and tap into what was going on. For all of the city's technology, Onyxia still had a raw natural side. He thrived in the dark dirty spaces. The earthy spaces where off worlders seemed like conspiracies.

That's how Zuri caught his attention. She spoke to him about nature and sound waves. He'd often sit in the window, watching her stretch and do her breathing exercises in the in the morning sun. She would always be nude. Her small perky body bending and contorting. Her breaths lifting and lowering her breast to the sky. He watched from his office, naked as well. He had learned to breathe as she would every day. Some mornings when the sun shone through his window heating his floor, he would slowly masturbate while he breathed along with her. Purposely moving his hands along his length. She had once told him "when breathing, focus on the feel of your heart beat. Treat it like a drum beating inside of your chest." It had taken him a bit of practice but one day he lay on his floor, naked, and masturbated to the feel and sound of his excited heartbeat. He didn't notice his own moans. The ejaculation was so powerful and the orgasm so intense. Isibo felt like he was in a trance. Ever since then, his sense of sound and touch were a bit different. More heightened.

He hung a small set of wind chimes just inside of the window to signal he may be present. They had an agreement, she didn't mind him watching as long as he used the chimes to announce his presence. She seemed too busy to notice him today, too busy hanging the small globes.

"Will you be going out tonight?" She asked over her shoulder, not bothering to look back.

"Yes. I have work."

"Come see me before you do. I would like to talk to you about something."

Zuri had her back to the door when Isibo walked in. Their apartments were connect by a private hallway that lead away from the other residents and commercial spaces in the building. She would leave the door unlocked for Isibo. She was wearing headphones and analyzing data. If not for the motion sensor that causes a green light to flicker she wouldn't have been aware of him. And even if she wasn't wearing the headphones she wasn't sure if she would have heard him. He moved like a ghost. He was sleek and graceful in his movements. Not like a dancer, but more like a fighter. She knew he would have closed the distance between her and the door before she turned around.

"I want you to listen to something." Zuri said, writing a final note on a pad before pressing a button on the bank of audio equipment. She turned her chair around and leaned back slightly. Isibo was dressed in a dark poncho that opened in the front and a body suit that fit snug against his body. She glanced up at him from her chair and suddenly felt sexually compromised. He wasn't a large man yet he seemed hard and imposing. Zuri let her mouth fall up thinking about him roughly feed his thickness to her.

"What am I listening to?" He asked leaning over the console, pulling her from her thoughts.

Zuri waved her hand. "Just listen."

She watched him stand again, fold his arms and close his eyes. He took three slow quiet deep breaths and paused.

"Zee, it's the sound of rain and a soft humming." Then he slowly up his eyes.

" what is that other sound, is it the city?"

Zuri smiled then shook her head.

"I think it's a language. I've been recording the rain for some time and recently I've been hearing more of that sound. It's a message; some kinda of language at least."

Isibo took the small controller and rewound the track to listen again. "Can you make a copy for me?"

"Yeah. And While you're out *working* can you see what the streets are saying, if anything about this?"

Isibo nodded his head. Zuri pulled the small chip free of the large console and handed it to Isibo. She stood hugged him and inhaled his scent. He smelled musky, strong and earthy. He smelled like an antique machine and masculine fragrance. This was another reason she was attracted to him. He was one of the few people, like her, who had stayed away from the technology enhancements that most of the population had received. Both Zuri and Isibo had older medical enhancements but no "veins" or biomechanical upgrades. He was old style. What they called a Dirt Man. She was a Dirt Woman. Because when they died their bodies would return back to the dirt. They both lived outside the system. This drew her to him.

(*Day 2 of Storm*)

Isibo squatted close to the fire that the small group of people had used to stay warm and dry in the tunnel beneath the old city. He had wanted to dismiss what Zuri had said about the "message" in the rain. It was easy to overlook what she said, even though he played the track repeated. The guttural whispers in the background of the sound slowly became the background for him over the last few days. There was talk of the storm; both underground and amongst the Corporate stations. Isibo wasn't able to tap into the rebel stations. The group was made up of a hodgepodge of people that formed a family. The Baron Joe was the Patriarch and leader of the family. He was a retired Soldier from the days when Countries were the lords of the lands. Once the Corporations took over, he and his kind were pushed out.

"The rain talks to me in my sleep." Baron Joe said crouching down to stoke the fire. The small group of people assembled around the fire nodded in unison.

"In what ways? What does it say." Isibo said, listening intently.

"Different things. For different reason. The biggest message is We have to prepare to be cleansed."

"Oba what about the flooding?" Unna the small young woman who acted as Baron Joe's granddaughter.

"Oh yeah *they* are going to flood the bugs away."

Isibo frowned.

"bugs…"? Isibo asked.

"Yes some folks have seen the tunnels under water in their dreams. Only thing is, all of us were bugs." Joe held his wrist up and tapped his veins. "It's easier to talk and understand if you had these."

Isibo looked at Baron Joe and nodded.

"You're right, but i don't and easier isn't better. So give me the dirty slow version." The Baron smiled and nodded his head in a rough agreement.

"The rain is talking to people. In a higher form of communication. It reminds me when we were first going off world. The communication feeds had a high frequency hissing that sounded like snakes. The brain folks told us it was nothing to worry about, but there was something there." Baron Joe mindlessly poked at the fire, looking into the flames as if he were talking to it and not Isibo. "But soldiers would complain about seeing snakes in their dreams. There was always a hissing sound. A lot of the soldiers said something was talking to them. Some would see snakes in their dreams. Some while they were awake, if you follow me. It is like that."

This was when he looked up at Isibo.

"I didn't listen then. But I'm listening now. I'm too old and scared to be stupid and brave. I'm taking my family in the mountains and waiting this storm out."

The two men shook hands and Isibo said his goodbyes. Baron Joe returned to preparing his family for moving out of the tunnels.

It was time to get out of the tunnels and back to work. Isibo watched different groups pack the pirate battery cells, weapons and food. Once he got out of the tunnels he nearly burst into a full sprint. The rain was coming down heavily and he wanted to get back to Zuri with his news.

"They had to prepare."

Isibo burst into Zuri's apartment expecting her to be sitting at her desk analyzing data from her test
He had been "working" and that took him into different parts of the city. Onxysia was quietly growing more frantic with chatter and movement. That chatter flowed through him. "It's definitely a language…" he started before registering that she wasn't sitting at her desk.
"Whoooaaaa Sir," Zuri said holding a large cup. She was wearing a soft pink robe, with a delicate spike on a leg holster. "You have to warn a lady." She smiled. The house was a bit warmer than the hallway. A heavy smell of scented oils and candles hung in the air. Isibo realized the room was dimmer than normal, seeing candles of varying sizes.
"You're soaked. Take these wet clothes off and tell me want you learned."
The sounds of the room slowly filled his head as he pulled wet clothing from his body. The sound of the rain was amplified and tuned. The background noises from before were now cleaner.
"There are multiple messages. Well two messages that repeat and the third is a constant tone. I think it a decoy or carrier

sound. It sounds like music so I've been listening to it more."

Zuri stood at the door of her bathroom, sipping tea and listening to Isibo recount his story. The soft pink *kasha fabric robe lay open, partly exposing her naked body underneath. The fine hair on her skin was standing, her nipples were erect and stiff beneath the soft then robe. Seeing him excited; turned her in so many ways. Not only was she captivated by his words but he had gotten caught in the storm and was soaked down to his underlining. As he talked he pulled the wet clothing from the his body. Now he stood, discussing the things he learned, fully erect. He mouth watered. His rough powerful smell called to her. She listened as he spoke about the dark dreams of the people and how some people were evacuating the city. She listened to his excitement but couldn't shake the thought of him stuffing her mouth.
"You should get in the shower."
Zuri had moved from the door to him, handed him her cup then dropped to her knees. "Keep talking." She slipped him into her mouth and inhaled his scent and taste. His strong body quivered from the heat of her mouth. She couldn't resist him. His flesh was a bit clammy a cold. She looked up at

him, into his eyes and saw a mixture of pleasured disgust. He felt like a guard towering over her. She moaned then whispered, "use me."

Although Isibo had bedded Zuri before something about how she acted was different. Her lustfulness was radiating from her. The "harmonic" sounds that floated through the room had his head throbbing. He felt intoxicated and powerful. He looked down at Zuri, seeing her hands around his girth. Her mouth looked too small to take all of him, but she opened mouth smoothly before sliding him into her warmth. He cursed and inhaled his own raw dirty smell. He frowned a bit then looked down at her. There was a mixture of powerful arousal and mild desire to degrade her. He heard her words, *use me,* and suddenly wanted to smash her like a bug. She seems so small and delicate. He slurped the warm tea into his throat and place the cup on desk. He bent forward forcing him thick length further down her throat. He pulled the robe's small belt free, grabbed her wrist, held them over her head and tied them together. Holding them over her head, Isibo used her wrist as handles, pounded himself in and out of her mouth. "You fucking dirty bug…".

Zuri's eyes slammed shut as Isibo pistoned in and out of her mouth. She heard the sounds of her own "gawking" and choking, accompanied by his degradation and the echo with in the rain. She felt passionate fluid running down her thighs as each rough penetration in to her mouth forced a "drop" to exit her lower vagina lips. She was overcome with the feeling of devoted usefulness as Isibo worked into her. She felt herself slipping into a dream where millions and millions of bugs were slowly crawling over her awakening her inner passions. Holding her bound hands in her grasp he sneered down at her calling her a bug. "A dirty fucking bug!"
She heard him (and the echo in the rain) say.

    Isibo felt like a passenger in his own body, as if he were looking at the world from a small command center in his head. He pulled his thick slobbery saliva covered member from Zuri's mouth. He still held her wrists in his hands. Outside, the force of the storm had increased so the sound was even more powerful. The ECHO felt like the original voice. He dropped her hands and grabbed her by her hair and lead her to the console. He bent her at the waist, grabbing a handful of her dainty buttocks, slid his hardness deep inside of her. His hips moved inside of her warm creaminess as they had for her mouth. Now she could actual use her voice. Each pant and moan was more urging to be used. To be dominated. *TO BE CONQUERED.* Isibo held one of her legs high in the air, with one hand and his hand on her neck with the other. There was an urging voice coming from the sounds of the rain to conquer her. Each thrust brought a deep gasp and pant from deep within her. He felt a deep and powerful wave growing inside of his gut. His muscles buzzed. Isibo had an intense sense of dominance coursing through him. They locked eyes and he suddenly knew she belonged to him. He tightened his grip around her throat. "I could break you, little bug." Her eyes rolled to the back of her head. She screamed just as thunder rumbled in the sky outside and the storm clouds inside of her released her own rain. Her fluids splashed against him. He released her throat and laid her flat in the desktop. There was a large candle on the console next to them. Isibo held the candle high and slowly poured the hot wax over her back and cheeks. A furiously passionate scream escaped her.

The relief Zuri felt was short lived. Isibo pulled himself free of her mouth. His meat bobbed at eye level covered in the saliva from deep within her throat. She was in a euphoric sexual storm. Juices flowed slowly from between her legs and a storm inside of her; matched the storm raging outside; both were commanding her to surrender and succumb to his power. She closed her eyes for a second and in a flash saw a flood running through the streets and overtaking her. Zuri took a quick breath as he grabbed her by her hair and pulled her to the desk. She felt him grab her throat and push inside. His thrust sounded like a monsters stomping through puddles. She felt him growing stiff and hard inside of her. With her mind's fingertips she rubbed the thick veins along his shaft. Working her internal muscles she caressed him with each thrust. His grip tightened around her throat. In that moment she knew she was his property. She felt powerless and loved it. "He could destroy me." He worked deeper and deeper inside of her, in unison with the storm. A growing pressure swelled in her. Suddenly the ECHO of the rain yelled inside of her mind, "FLOOD THE TUNNELS!" and a warm, bright and silent flash went in her mind. The her orgasm rushed from her and all over him. Zuri felt a dream like sluggish come over her. He rolled her flat on stomach; still in side of her but moving slowly. The ECHO whispered to her to prepare. And without warning the intense heat of the candle wax covered her back and ass cheeks. A violent orgasm rippled from her soul, through her body. She screamed loudly and passionately; standing on her tip toes. Then the feeling of him releasing hot life streams back into her. Zuri cursed and stretched her hands out to the rain for relief. Isibo grabbed her again by the hair. He pulled him self free of her loins, spun her around then fed himself to her. Zuri kneeled at his feet and suckled on his slowly softening meat. She drank of him until he crumbled to his knees and pulled her into an embrace.

The apartment was quiet except for the storm raging outside of the windows. They lay in deep silence.

"What do you think that was about?" Isibo asked. Zuri lying with in his arms, head against his chest.

"I think our inner desires were amplied. I felt compelled to be conquered. But i also felt sexually hungry for you." She said then laughed. "You called me a bug."

A bit of embarrassment seeped out of Isibo with a soft exhale.

"But i have never enjoyed the sound of the bug more in my life." She rubbed her flaccid length and smiled.

"Do you think it was the message in the rain?" He asked

"Yes and no. Yes there is a message being sent and it may very well have subliminal messages. But no the bedding was more or less us. Again I think what ever the message is in the rains echo amplifies the desires already. I didn't have a need or wish to resist you. I just wanted to be conquered."
"I felt the opposite. I wanted to dominate you and crush you like a bug. It just manifested this way."
"What if I had resisted…"
" i felt compelled to break any resistance…" Isibo trailed off. They both suddenly understood want that meant. They both silently thought about what it meant for the rest of the city. Bugs would scurry and resist. They be crushed and stamped out. And those that ran into tunnels to hide would be drown and flushed out. Zuri crawled atop of Isibo and kissed him.
"We must prepare. They are coming."
He nodded his head in the darkness.
"Then we will be prepared."

Lighting's Lover

Neko stood beneath the jungles canopy and scanned the area around him. Even with all of his enhancements and electrical harnessing upgrades eblast bullets were still a very real threat. He was the most vulnerable when he activated his E.F.S. (Electric Field Sensors). Once he found the right spot he could handle the power surges that coursed through him and his suit. What he couldn't handle was the guards and their guns. Being this close to the SilcoLabs power fields was always a dangerous task. He had one more large order to fill before he could return to the city. So the smart thing was to sit tight and monitor the communications waiting for the right time. Usually doing this allowed him the opportunity to harvest more than just electricity. Secrets were a high commodity. He overheard everything from routine transmissions like supply deliveries and daily announcements. Today was shark and yams. Neko missed having roasted yams and fish with Kali. She was an impeccable cook. Her cooking always made him feel like nestling into warm plushiness. He leaned back against a tree and thought of his former lover. Thought of her embrace. Thought of her bosom. Smiled thinking of their releases. Neko made a point to himself to try and contact her again as some chatter came through the ultra secret lines. One of the benefits of being an Electricity Harvester was that he could decipher any encrypted message that he was already monitoring.

"Project Storm is confirmed. Direct all Upper Management personnel to have vaccination and debugging program virus downloaded NLT 0900…" some one Neko recognized as a high level officer, said.

The responder replied a tad bit confused.

"Sir is this a secure line?"

"Yes this line is clean…"

" what does all of this mean?"

The high ranking officer exhaled in frustration then replied.

"Captain… just have your staff get the enhancement vaccine uploads. The storm that's coming is going to have some embedded…"

The transmission was cut short. Neko was alerted to a patrol team in his area. He switched his systems to defense and disconnected from his gear. He could return in a few days to get the equipment he needed later. He knew he needed to send the information he had to someone who could use it.

A day later

Neko walked into a small flower shop and smiled at the clerk. He was a young man with a somewhat pleasant yet rough disposition. The kind that told Neko the clerk had a different life before finding work at the flower shop. He knew the clerk had been placed in the shop by the rebellion as security for the "cafeteria" that had been set up here. Usually there was a woman who was much more pleasant working the counter leaving this guy, Terrance, to do the labor and more physical things. Neko made the necessary checks to ensure the shop was safe to place his orders. He grabbed two bags of potting soil and seeds, which was a sign that he was sending a message. The conversation would have an actual message and its recipient laced in.
"Did you find everything you needed?" Terrance said as he rang the items up.
"Yeah. Most things anyway. Quick question do you all have the health care almanac here? There's a storm coming that has me kinda nervous about getting sick and so I wanted to get ahead of it."
"Not now. But I can place an order."

"That would be great. Can you place a rush on it. I'll pay extra to get in sooner. It may rain in a couple weeks and I wanna be safe by then. I normally let my sister do it since she is a nurse. It's harvesting time. I try to be very careful with it. Having the right herbs just boosts my bodies general defenses. And that's very important to me. The stuff they have at these corporate stores scare me. Ya never know what they trying to put in our food and water." Neko trailed off and smiled.

Without looking up, the clerk Terrance, chuckled, "yeah you never know what they are doing. Do you want to leave a deposit. Or a tip?" That's when the clerk looked up to make brief eye contact

"Yes. Put both on my account and max the tip."

Neko extended his hand. The clerk nodded and dapped with Neko before exchanging a quick shake.

(Two weeks before the storm)

The women stood in a loose circle staring at the larger of them. The rebellion had been lead by five women known as the Udugu or Sisterhood. Each of them held the rank of general and command of a different faction. Sister Meeka was the General of the Medical Corps. Sister Yazmin was the General of

Finance. Sister Linda was the General of Diplomatic Affairs. Sister Shaw was the General of Communication and Education. And Sister Kali was the General of Defense. Normally the five women wouldn't meet together in the same place. Sister Shaw called the secret meeting as a sign of importance. With the storm as powerful as it was for the last couple of days, the authorities and Corporations were too to busy to track them. Also Sister Shaw needed the Sisters in attendance to help her convince Kali to speak to her ex-boyfriend. Shaw needed equipment for the

"No! Do not ask me to deal with that grimey slug." Kali spat. She held on to the large leashes of her two hounds. Her heart pounded and her stomach turned. Rage boiled inside of her.

"Sister,"it was Meeka who spoke. "If there was a different way, I would have done it. He is the only Harvester with the packs for the hospital equipment. We even offered to pay twice as much for the gear. I spoke with him after his request from the flower shop."

Kali tugged at the leashes. The hounds whined and pulled at the end of the chains.The women in the room were the only people Kali allowed to fed them treats.

"He said he had some important information that he would only give to you. He requested a secret TALK IN PERSON meeting. I couldn't go even if I wanted to. He wants you."

" I could send a team of raiders and they could get the gear and extract the information." Kali said. She had made it a point to not see Neko. It was just like him to play these games. In her mind there was nothing she had to say to him. Well almost nothing. She thought as the feeling and memories of being a top of him ran through her mind.

"Please go see the man," it was Linda. She laughed and walked over to the hounds, pulling treats from her pocket to feed them, then rubbed their large heads. "You know you miss him and I'm tired of you acting like you don't want him in your bed."

The women laughed. It was settled Kali would go meet with the Harvester.

(Two days later)

Neko adjusted his suit and tried his best not to fidget or seem nervous. He had been trying to find ways to meet with Kali. To explain to her he was sorry and that he had changed. But he understood breaking a woman's heart isn't something you can just apologize for and things are fixed. Especially when that woman goes off to become the

General of an actual rebel army. Although he had a squad of his own, he knew that there was no comparison. He needed a real reason to contact her. An even more real reason for her to respond kindly. Last time she saw him she released her hounds on him. Had it not been for his suit and power rod, things may have been bad. He needed leverage. It wasn't until the Sisters needed the power packs and other gear for the hospitals and camps did he see his chance. Having intercepted information about the SincoLabs' plans, gave him all he needed to have her come to him. Leverage!

"She's here!" One of the watchmen called back to him. Neko nodded that he was ready to receive her. He moved to the front of his desk and smiled.

"Let her in and leave us be." Neko said to the watchman, who nodded and smiled.

"General," he said as Kali walked past him, holding the leashes in her hand. The two hounds were free to roam but stayed by her side. As the door closed behind her, Kali whispered roughly, "WATCH", to the hounds, whose ears perked up, then both sniffed small areas near the door on either side and laid just inside of the door.

"Now we are safe and secure," Kali said, walking toward Neko. "What is this message you want to discuss?"

Her stance was strong and defiant. It had been some time since they both had seen each other and things had definitely changed. Physically they both looked differently. Neko could see that the days had been a bit harsher on her face but her body was now the polished body of a sultry soldier. He could see her outline through her clothing. Gone was the pudgy softness of his griot ex girl friend. Now stood a beautifully tall alluring sentry of a woman. "There is an impending storm coming. The Corporation has a scheme to take over the people and eradicate the population…" he trailed off. "You look lovely Ma'Kali. I've missed you." And before he could finish Kali had quickly closed the distance between them and grabbed Neko by the throat. "I don't need your sentimental words Harvester." She sneered. She could feel the heat of his blood and a small pulse of electricity running through his body. She stared deep into his eyes. "Im no longer the soft woman you said could do with out. I'm now the General of a strong Army. I could kill you and your men with just one word. I could tie you to that table and torture you." Kali felt a new surge of Domineering power flowing through her. She had thought about what she would do if she had finally gotten her hands on Neko. She played the thought of hurting him in the way that he hurt her. She dreamt of tying him to a post, spread eagle, and allowing her hounds to devour him, starting at his loins. She would snickering at the thought of him on his knees screaming in pain and begging for his life. The very next intrusive thought was how much she missed him being inside of her. Neko had always been a passionate and attentive bed mate. He always pleasured her with both his loins and his greedy mouth. He would lap at her wetness like and little hound pup. That was how she became such a great trainer of hounds. She thought about how much she would train Neko if he were her little pet. She trained her hounds to be loyal and obedient. To be at her call whenever she needed them. And although the hounds kept her warm they were not a man. She could not bed them. And now finally her diabolical dreams were true. She would make Neko get on his knees and beg her for his life. Then he would show his devotion.

Kali slapped Neko across the face. She smiled as her body began to awaken with pleasure pulsing through her muscles.

"If you miss me so much Harvester. I want to you get undressed and kneel at my feet and beg for my forgiveness. Be a good hound

and show me how much you deserve to
live."

Neko did his best to stay calm. Kali had
surprised him with her quickness. She
caught him off guard and was a lot stronger
and meaner than he remembered. She was
right. She was no longer the soft woman he
knew. She was a fighter now. Her hands
were around his throat and cutting both;
blood flow and air flow to his brain. She
could end with ease. This thought sent a
deep pulsating feeling through him. His brain
began registering the bio electrical energy
radiating from Kali. Neko would do anything
to taste her. Her slapping him across the
face was a fierce delight. Neko wanted to
make amends for things and this was more
than he had hoped. He pulled the suit from
his body, exposing the veins running over
his body, connected to the other
enhancements and cybernetic parts of him.
As he kneeled, it was obvious to Kali that he
had changed as well. She slowly walked
around him admiring, inspecting and
marveling at his body. His left thigh was an
energy channel prosthetic. She noticed the
"veining" run over his muscles and limbs
were thicker than others. There was actual
circuitry intertwined. Neko dipped his head

and smiled. Kali stood in front of him and placed her hand on his head.

"Show me you miss me. Be a good hound and kiss my boots."

Neko did as he was told and began kissing her black shiny boots. Gently and slowly at first. Something in her voice set his arousal on fire. The sounds of his kisses were loud and exaggerated. Kali smiled down at him, feeling small tremors run through her body with each "smooch". He even pushed a deep moan from his throat as his mouth moved across her boots.

"Now… I want to hear you beg for your life and for my forgiveness."

Neko cleared his throat and nestled his face lower to her boots. He kissed and pleaded with Kali. "Please Maam don't kill me." He begged. "I'll be a good boy this time. I'll do whatever you wish."

Kali listened to his words and wanted to humiliate and degrade him. She thought about how his lies felt like he had taken a piss on her and she wanted to return the favor.

"Kneel with your arms behind your back. I want you to drink my piss, so you know how it feels to be pissed on and lied to."

Kali pulled the front of her dress up slight and grabbed and tugged at her underwear until they were at her ankles, stepped out of them; skillfully stepped free. Rolling the the rest of her dress up, she bent her right knee and placed it on his shoulder, then pulled his head slightly forward. She had learned sometime ago to go standing up. As a soldier she couldn't get caught with her pants down. She was always on alert. Kali leaned down to spit in his face a second before a hard stream splashed against his face. A surprising arousing sexual disgust swept through her as she watched him open his mouth. She pulled him tightly against her body hoping to drown him slightly. The heat from his mouth nearly made her knees buckle. He drank from her fountain. He wrapped his lips around Venus gently sucked the last of her piss. Her eyes rolled backward in her head a his tongue rolled over her buzzing mother pearl. Kali grimaced and cursed with passion. She heard his pleas in between the moans and slurps. "Please let be your good boy." Leaning backward, Kali placed her hand on the table behind her and slowly crawled atop; pulling him along. Sitting up to stare down at him lapping greedily at her juices. She had sworn off men and intimate touch since their last encounter years ago, and she was now drunk with the power of watching Neko lick and slurp at her command. His tongue obeyed her panted commands. She stopped to randomly to slap or spit in his face calling him her good boy. Neither she nor Neko noticed that hos body was sending a low voltage surge through her. Each touch of his touch and finger tips sent actually volts of electricity pulsing through their bodies. So when he moved his hand from her thigh, to her stomach, his thumbs was close enough to her clitoris for a small arc of electricity to jump back and forth between the points of contact. Kali was literally shocked into another powerful orgasm sending new fluids deep from within her. The subsequent fluids carried sparks creating a sexual electro-rainstorm between the two of them. For what seemed like an eternity the of them were stuck together shaking and writhing about. Both moaning and grimacing. Once the sensation ended, Neko fell back to the floor lying in a small puddle, panting. Kali sat up dizzy and powerfully aroused, a new hunger had been awakened in her. Her body still buzzed as she sat forward and saw his large fat erection pointing to the ceiling. She scooted to the edge of the table and nearly leaped directly atop of him. She straddled, then eased him into her wetness. She exhaled sharply from the feeling of is electrified meat pulsing; encouraging her insides to continue pulsating. She placed both feet to each side and slowly bounced on him. Now she could really feel the electric sensation. This was new for her. She had heard that he had an accident and was augmented and enhanced. "Your exlover is the Lightning Harvester", they would tell her as his reputation grew. She didn't know that meant he actually held electricity in his body. She gripped his neck squeezing firmly and moved slowly up and down his lighting rod. She felt the slightly more than gentle electro-therapy flowing through her sexual self. She also took on all the downloads. She saw the secret message about the impending storm. She saw his pain after the accident. She saw the transformation in his mind, heart, and his deep depression. She transmitted her anger and grief after their breakup. The joy and pain of becoming a rebel and moving up the ranks. They both transmitted their lust for the other.

Neko slowly moved his hands over Kali's body, bringing a small sexual lightning storm to different regions of her body. The sweat moistened her skin expanding the reach of the sparks. Her thighs as she shifted from her feet to her knees, shifting her weight and the positioning. With her body in full contact with his body, the externally sensation decreased but the internal sensation increased. Their mixture of fluids gave the sparks waves to ride and explore. Her heart felt out of sync until she realized she had synced to his. Kali moved her hands from his neck to his chest, teasing the exposed circuitry of his veins. She quickly slapped him and cursed.

"Open!" She said with one word command. Neko opened his mouth as she forced a stream of his thick sweet saliva to flow from her mouth to his. And just as it touched his tongue slower surge of electricity ran from his mouth and up into and down to her womb. Every muscle in her body contracted as he pushed upward into and again a sexual electric circuit was completed. The force moved and threw Kali around as dual waves or juices; both wet and electric flowed out of her, down over him and suddenly around them. In an instance, they exchanged every thought and memory the other had. His secrets were her secrets and hers were now his. This was a new bond. The force shut her mind down and forced her to collapse on top of him.

The entire time she never heard him as he continued to beg to be forgiven.

Sometime later Kali was awaken by the texture of her hounds licking her face. She wasn't sure how long she was out. She was lying on a raised platform with mats under a blanket filled with his scents.

"I sent word for food to be brought." He smiled from his chair next to the platform. "Your team has secured the perimeter and my team has set up surveillance General. You're safe here with me."

Kali sat up, disregarding the fact she was now completely naked. "Thank You Harvester. We can discuss the storm after we eat. My sisters will be able to get the word out."

Neko whistled a short harmonious burst, calling both hounds to his feet.

Kali sat up, shocked, then smiled.

"I would like to talk about US FIRST." Neko said closing the door. "I need US again."

Kali nodded her head in agreement. "Okay. Let's discuss us."

4.Rain Dancer's Enigma

Detective Ravina Tau didn't need to be a detective of 13 years to know this crime scene wasn't correct. It wasn't the crowd of people who were different versions of the same person. It wasn't the glowing aura of light softly radiating from the victim's corpse. Nor was it the her point of view, floating above the entire scene. It was the sound of Armon Charles, crying softly in her ear, saying he needed her. That he didn't feel safe and only she could help him. The sound of him crying filled her with a deep fright. That's how she knew this wasn't real. That this was all a dream. The other give away was the fear she felt. She was never frightened or scared at crime scenes. Even if a perp had returned, they rarely attacked anyone. They watched from the crowd. Crime scenes in general were the safest places to be, in her opinion. They were filled with eager police officers ready to be heros. It was that deep sense of fear radiating Armon, as well, that concerned her. His deep fear told her something was wrong and abnormal. Which meant she was dreaming. Armon sobbed heavily. "This rain is rotten Tau. It isn't natural. It's poison. The rain is poison. It's infested." He said, in the previous dreams. Only now he was crying. Weeping actually. She was never clear what rain Armon was talking about because there was never any rain in her dreams. There was no rain in this crime scene. She listened to his sobbing from somewhere in her subconscious.

"Save me Dectective Tau. Save me from this poison. From this infestation".

Ravina shot up in her hover bed, face wet from her own tears and sweat. Her nipples were sore from being stiffened due to the cold fright she felt. She held her eyes closed for a few moments longer before clicking into the weather feed. There was no indication of any bad weather for a few weeks. It wasn't strange that Armon could accurately predict the rain. He had done it before. This time he wasn't predicting rain. During their relationship he would tell her a lot about rain and the weather. He spoke about it in a grand mystical way. Spoke about the alignment of planets, currents of the sea and moons. Spoke to her about how it would affect people and animals. How her cycle could be affected. And when it rained he could read people's minds and spirits. A few times when she had a case weighing on her mind, he could tell her if a person she had interviewed was lying or if she was going in the wrong direction. For her, him speaking about rain wasn't strange; not even in her dreams. What was strange was there was no rain in the forecast and they hadn't spoken in three years. Armon had told her, his "touch" wasn't strong unless he actually touched someone or if he was searching for them. Or if it rained. "Maybe", she thought quietly in the darkness of her bedroom, "he had gotten stronger."

She eased back into the comfort of bed and laid there thinking of his touch on her body. She stuffed a pillow between her legs, bunched her large warm weighted blanket on top of that, then exhaled and welcomed the feeling of something being on top of her. She monitored her breathing, wishing Armon was there to comfort her. In her dreams he needed her help. But here in the waking world, even as a Detective she wanted and needed him and his unique style of comfort. She thought about how he would touch her. He was the person who taught her to appreciate her body; especially her breast. Her breast weren't big by any means. They were, on her most bloated days, no more than a hand full. Armon had a way of moving his long fingers down the sides of her body, with his thumbs on top. He would slide his thumbs under the curvature of her breast, bringing his fingers up along her sides.

"Your nipples look like they're floating on your beautiful brown skin."
Times like now she would lick her fingers and try her best to mimic the movements of his tongue. She remembered him telling her to think of the most romantic version of rain. "Think of the smell and sound of it in your mind." She heard him saying from the past. Ravina wrapped her legs around the blanket bundles and thought of the smell of rain. She gently tweaked and rolled her nipples, pressing her pelvis up into the pillow. She thought of the rain drenching her body. She reached out with her mind into the darkness for his energy and he reached back. She lost track of her hands. She only thought of his warmth and the rain that swarmed in her mind and deep within her body. She wasn't sure when the release had come but she suddenly felt relaxed. The small puddle beneath her slowly growing cold. She had let the mental rain clouds go away. Ravina stood at the foot of her bed, stretched and decided to find Armon's information and go see him.

That was roughly a month ago This current storm had swept over the city and although storms in Onyxsia were common this storm had been going for days and things seem different. When the storms began being broadcast across the different channels, thoughts of Armon seeped into her brain.

Something about this storm was simply off.

"This rain stinks. Smells rancid." Patrolman Justice said, holding out a cup of chai for Detective Tau.

"What did you say," Tau asked turning toward the patrolman.

"This rain stinks. It smells rancid. Almost like it's poisoned. This is probably why people have been acting doofy lately."Ptlman Justice said sipping his hot drink. "What do you think happened here." Justice pointed down at the nude bodies of the two women. The women were found in the alley by a taxi driver who pulled over to relieve himself.

"I'm not sure yet," Tau said feeling her spirit stepping outside of her body. She watched herself say the rest from what felt like an aura filled booth. Her words sounded as if she were listening underwater. "It looks like they were killed somewhere else and dumped here. they look like dolls."

Tau tilted her head and looked at the bodies. The two women had flawless skin. They looked manufactured and plastic. Too beautiful to be from here. This city or this planet. It was then Tau noticed they didn't have veins. Their skin seemed synthetic. Neither of them had public hair. Their breast, all four, seemed perfectly symmetrical. All the same size and level of perkiness. She had heard of cybernetically enhanced people but they generally lived Off-World or were high-end companions to the Ultra Wealthy. Someone would eventually come looking for them. Ravina floated about the scene on an astral level. She watched patrolman Justice sip from his cup. Justice's words were distant and cloudy. The words were only important to Tau in that physical world. Here, her spiritual self was focused on other things. She stood in the same alley from her dreams. No sobbing Armon. Now instead of physical bodies, she could see the energetic presence; their *Ka*(pronounced KAH, their total life force). Armon had taught her to see their auras. As well as feel and hear their vibrational waves. Normally the colors were soft whites, or vibrant blues and violets. The sounds were harmonic and beautiful. Now she noticed the colors were a bit faded and putrid. She saw the rain appeared dirty and stained a of the clouds were polluted. The drops felt oily. The smell was rancid.

"Touch the bodies, Tau". Armon's powerfully soothing voice, started her on this plane causing her physical body to shudder. "Touch the bodies so that I can see through the rain." She looked at the two bodies. The

Ka appeared like a fading neon bulb. Different from the other people in attendance. (Ravina sensed a powerful warm blank spot just pasted the people. For a brief moment it grew from warm to hot then warm again.) On the physical plane, Ravina sipped roughly from her cup and walked over to the bodies. She placed her cup down next to the closest of the two, then reached out her gloveless had and touch the first body's then placed her hand on the fore arm of the other body. She could she Armon now. She saw where his physical body was located. She saw his slender form standing in the shower naked, his meat semi filled with excite dangling between his legs. He saw through her and into the women. He saw their last moments and who they spent those moments with. He saw the alley. Showed her where possible clues were and then he saw her seeing him.

"Come see me Tau. These women are not from this planet." He whispered as he left her. "Come see me."

Ravina blinked a few quick times then looked around again. She fought off shock and confusion. For those looking on no time had truly passed. It was barely noticeable. But for Ravina the exchange felt like an eternity. She slowly gathered her self and stood. She quickly instructed the investigation team on where and what to look for, telling them nothing more than "it seems important" and "bag, label, catalogue everything before the rain ruins our evidence." She watched them work before slowly fading into the background and turning the scene over to a junior detective.

Dr. Esteban Stone, The CEO of The Tyzine Corporation, stood in the red dimly lit room within his private quarters. The room was a large featureless dungeon-like open space on his space craft. The Galactic Cruiser, orbited the planet in stealth mode. He had been overseeing the HIVE weather project from here and finally had some time to unwind. His eyes were closed and he channeled his deep tantric breathing. Space travel could take a toll on humans bodies. Some people had been driven mad and lost control of their mental health due to the bending and warping of time.
"*You are free*." A gentle slightly robotic female humanoid voice whispered from the dark. "*You are free*". Doctor Stone open his to see his cybernetic concubine "Ester 6K" suspended by drone restraints, from her limbs in a spread eagle style "X". Her deep purple skin looked pitch black in the hue of the red light. She was crafted and enhanced to physically complement Stone's massive

statue. Stone was 8 lengths tall and 21.5 stones. And very sadistic. He needed a companion who could withstand his force. Ester 6K was the perfect companion. She was 6 lengths and 18 stones. Her outer fleshy body was voluptuous and curvy. She had been compromised of females from multiple species; human, Gharvelian (harpy like creatures) and an unnamed insect species from a newly discovered galaxy. His scientists had learned that the species had a few characteristics that communicated with a hive like telepathy and possessed a very active rejuvenating genes. Its had taken some experimental trials to perfectly blend species(approximately 6,271) until the perfect model was achieved. Now he had a perfectly subservient masochistic slave who would protect him and craved his vile and evil treatment as a means of endearment. The whispering that happened in his head was simply a way to nurture the small part of him that cared if he was a good man. It was an acknowledgment that he was free of such emotions. The freedom to be a sadist who gifted her with extreme pain. Pain was the Prize. "Pain is Love",

Ester whispered in his mind. She lifted her head slightly revealing her glowing eyes. She saw him unfurl the long whip made of Dragon scale and starsmetal.

Doctor Stone gave the handle of the whip a small flick sending ripples through it, until the small claw on the end of the whip "clinked" against the warm metal floor. He exhaled, pulled the whip up and around his head into a full circle then brought it down and outward striking Ester across her exposed torso, slicing her open with the scale's razor sharp edges before quickly pulling it backward and repeating the motion. She wailed in pleasure. Her long tail flopped behind her in glee. Esteban grinned in sadistic pleasure; his thick and heavy unit grew with each lash. He actually envied her tail and sent a lash across her face, in a spiteful sadistic lusting because of his envy. Smiling as she wailed, he moved to send another lash when a low chime sounded behind his left ear where the small communication button sat. The only person who would dare to disturb him was his assistant and second in command; Darnesha Payne.

"We have an issue that requires your immediate attention Sir."

"Continue with the details", he said frustrated at the disturbance.

"There seems to have been some miscalculations with the JUMP team. Dr. Stone…" his cybernetically enhanced assistant, Darnesha Payne said, over the secure pirated signal. "It seems they were separated; two of them have been found dead. The third's location has not yet been determined."

His assistant downloaded the report to his feed. It seemed the three person JUMP team had been sent off course. It seems none of the planning team had foresaw more powerful lighting and the electromagnetic fields would affect them. He sneered in the darkness. These miscalculations were not acceptable. He tapped the top of his left wrist, signaling the restraining drones to lower Ester to the room's deck.

"Please observe the investigation. Dispatch a team to locate and recover the third member. I will be there shortly. And Miss Payne, please ensure all calculations are correct moving forward."

"Yes Doctor."

"Now sync me into the communications there so I can monitor things."

Ravina walked down the long hallway studying the dancer studio's marketing posters. It was clear that Armon and his dance group had been busy since they last shared space. Even the building it self had undergone some upgrades. The old warehouse space with its dark and dank appearance had become retrofitted and illuminated. Detective Tau laughed to herself, thinking how unsafe it appeared, all along she was hosting a self defense class for citizens. It was how she and Armon met. She needed a space for her classes and her urban tactics training and he needed paying customers.

"If you teach me to defend myself, Detective, I'll teach you to dance. Or atleast help you improve your footwork."

Ravina thought of those times as she walked past the dance spaces. The exchange of intimate energy and information. She could feel his hands on her back, pressing her against his body. He was a lean, yet deceptively strong and solid man. When they dance he moved her body with his body's movement. She quickly learned that he didn't need her to show him how to defend himself. He would twirl her, use the momentum to sweep her off of her feet, then place her delicately back to the floor. It always took her breath away. He was what he called a Rain Fighter. It was a form of dances that could be also used as a fighting style. He showed her how to dance and they would spar-intimate and artistically. Tau walked further into the building, coming to a large studio. She could her hi tapping his large staff against the flow and counting down. She pushed into the room, hoping to go unnoticed. Armon stood facing the group of dancers, and noticed Ravina walk into the room from his right.

"Although the movements have to be in sync as if each dancer is moving in precision to the others, please do not overthink things. Feel the music. The steps will come if you flow with the music." Armon walked over to one of his assistants, whispered into her ear, causing the assistant to look at Ravina and smile. The assistant received the small staff and he turned his attention to Ravina Tau. "Detective you look beautiful." He hugged her then whispered. "Thank you for coming. I have a lot to show you."

   Michasha(Mee KAH shuh)"Micha" Ellington sat at her desk, pretending to read files and care about the processing the forensic files. Working the late dark moon shift, allowed her to work in a less busy time of the day. Tonight she simply wanted to take her time not doing anything. Her vacation was starting in a day. She would be on the sunny side of the globe, far away from Onyxsia and this rain. Something was wrong with this storm and she wanted to be somewhere else until it was over. She only had to process the rush file; two women found dead in an alley in the Gold Hills area of the city. There was a note stating a detective, Ravina Tau, would be in later in the day to investigate and review the bodies. Michael just needed to organize the notes from the senior coroner. She could do that after she shopped for her vacation. Just then a slight knock at the door alerted her to someone entering into the lab. She looked up in time to see three men; two soldiers and a large deep brown tone, monster of a man in a surprisingly tailored three piece suit. His smile reminded her of the child's tale of a wolf that lured children to eat candy with him.

"Miss Ellington, I presume." Dr. Stone said. Micha looked up, locked eyes and slowly nodded in affirmation. "I'm Doctor Esteban Stone. I'm the CEO of The Tyzine Corporation, a Chair on the InterGalactic Network of Planets." He held up a badge with I.D. that seemed very official.

"How may I help you?" She did her best to appear brave and professional. However there was an overwhelming sense of fear and deep arousal. He moved like a mystical being but the size of beast.

"You have two bodies that are a part of an investigation that we are here to recover them." Before Micha could process the words, one of the soldiers presented a small stack of documents. She smiled at the three men; nervous yet compliant. Micha felt a weirdly powerfully frighten arousal as she stared at the big one, Dr. Stone. Her sexual appetite grew. She felt as if he could read her thoughts. She wanted them gone as soon as possible. Dr Stone stared deep inside of her. His expression never changed. "I would do what ever this man commanded of me," she thought.

Breaking eye contact, Micha took the paperwork from the soldier, filled out the appropriate forms and called the release station. She was happy to be done with the ordeal. She watched them leave with two bodies and a sense of relief swept over her. Now her vacation could start.

(An hour off she was sure they were gone, Michasha masturbated at the thought of Dr. Stone slowly guiding her mouth over his hardened length. It was thick dark and veiny. Then him bending her over her desk and powerfully filling her womb. She thought she dreamt it. Even telling her friend that she had dreamt it. "It felt so real." She didn't tell her that she felt hands on her body. Nor did she tell her friend that she had released harder than she had ever done in her life. There was a small puddle on the floor. She thought about Dr. Stone while on her vacation as well.)

Armand led Detective Tau to the roof of his building. The roof had been reconstructed and a small wooden deck had been built, allowing guest to sit and enjoy the night sky. The rain had subsided to a steady drizzle. The air was cool and wet. Just to the other side of the deck was an area with a large screen covering a lounge space. There were drums and large throw pillows, and other plush chairs and rugs. It sat off I the corner of the roof in a space that sat in the shadows of a neighboring building, giving Ravina a sense of seclusion and secrecy. She watched him walk toward the space and begin undressing. Without words, she took his cue and began undressing as well. She kept her eyes on his naked body as he stepped from beneath the screen,into the rain, allowing the drizzle to run against and down his body. She slowly pulled the clothing from her body; watching him the entire time.

"Come dance with me," he held his hand out to her. Although he smiled his face was very solemn and pleasantly stern, yet reassuring. Ravina stepped free of her sock, tossing it to the pile of clothing, then gingerly hopped via her tiptoes, grabbed his hand and allowed him to pull her close, twirl her smoothly then pulled her right into him. His body was much hotter in temperature than she anticipated.

His passion warmed them both. He felt feverishly hot against her cool skin. She felt his length growing more rigid and in warmth against her skin.

"What do you want to show me?" She asked, her head lay against his chest.

"I want you to listen to the rhythm of the rain. Listen to the voices and you'll understand."

Ravina inhaled deeply and tried to block out the sounds of the city. Then after a few intense breaths she heard his voice; not from outside of her but from deep within her. "Don't listen with your ears and hear. Listen with your heart and your soul. Let your primal lustful desire translate the rains rhythm and voice." She eased a heavy breath from deep inside of her. Then suddenly a rush of warm syrupy sensations introduced themselves to her senses. The sound of the rain was a jaggedly angelic aural harmony. It was seductively haunting. The drops that hit her skin felt oily yet it had a sweet taste. She turned her eyes to look at the droplets and could see a light rainbowesque swirling of colors just below the surface. The smell was devilishly sweet and inviting. The type of invite that came with a seductive stipulation. With each breath, she was brought deeper and deeper into the new place.

"Do you understand now?" Armand asked as he moved her about, dancing in this ethereal place. She nodded her head.

"What is that? What's happening?" She asked feeling more and more- influenced.

"It's the rain. The rain is contaminated"

"How?"

"I'm not sure. Maybe We can find out together."

Ravina smiled, lifting her face to the sky. The voice and rhythm of the rain spoke to her primal side. She felt deeply and lustfully animalistic. She felt her actual body moving in step with his, but her spiritually tantric danced to and ravenous sound. Her hips moved against his called for his body. Armand placed his hand on her left thigh gently guiding her into her, but Ravina tossed her leg around his waist, and tipped her head backward. This caused them to spin. He placed his hand at her lower back just as she tossed the other leg around his waist, surprising them both. The rains sound urged their movements. A deep guttural chanting could be heard. And a sound she first believed was whispered but learned with each movement was hissing. Armand dipped forward with her, then bite her neck passionately, before pulling her upright and into him. Ravina dug her nails across his back. She wanted to devour him. And be devoured by him. In this dreamscape, the voice and music of the rain became an elixir and she became very intoxicated. She pulled herself into him then slowly slithered her legs over his shoulders. She crossed her ankles and held his head as Armand gently kissed her moist center. Ravina tilted her head back closing her eyes and listened to the rain's intoxicating song. As his toughest moved over her body she could hear in her head.

"I must devour you…" he hissed and moaned. Keeping her head back, she rolled her hips and pelvis. She told her body to open up to him. To flood his mouth with her juices, like a tunnel.

The more she rolled her his, gyrating against his tongue, the lower her body slipped to the roof; upside down. Ravina placed her hands on the wet surface, a foot on his chest-steadied herself there for a few more licks, then flipped completely over. She looked at him, coming face to face with his stiffness, bobbing erect between his legs. She moved -slithered- to him, slowly swallowing him bite by gentle bite like a serpent swallowing an egg. By now the rain increased past a drizzle. The music it made, with the voices it was infused with sounded like a demonic tantric choir. Ravina worked her mouth deep and slowly over him, filling her mouth with him until they both irked and jerked from the sensation. Her body buzzed and itched. Her passion rose as the rain ran over her body like bugs crawling over her skin. He pushed in a rhythmic dance inside of her mouth. The dance they were doing now felt like in was ingrained in them. Ravina felt like she was being rewired. Being pirated now. The rain ran down her back, between her cheeks, and continued into to her small erect button. Each drop feeling like an erotically deviant bug. And there felt like hundreds of drops. Rain over her breast. Rain over her feet and between her toes. She felt covered in them. The feeling began driving her mad with ecstasy. She could feel him growing powerfully rigid in her mouth. Like she was swallowing a warm blooded snake. Ravina felt her eyes itching. It was at his moment Armand looked down at her, possessed by the rain and looked into her eyes; seeing them change like those of a serpent. He pushed backward from her, freeing himself from her mouth, seeing a long serpent tongue wrapping it self around his length before closing his eyes and letting the rain take them.

Ravina never felt more out of control. Yet she never in her life wanted to be controlled more than now. She felt Armand urging her in her mind. Her pulled her to stand. Doing as she was told, her pulled her right leg up and around her waist, dipping her backward he slipped into her. Ravina bent completely backward and gave herself to his dance. This Dirty Rain dance. She was in a complete backbend, palms on the roof while he held the other leg in the air, working deeper into her. Ravina trembled and shook upside down. "*They are using the rain to control us*,"she thought. She knew this now. This understanding came to her. This is what Armand wanted to show her. Then a sudden dark presence over came her a moment. A deep guttural voice hissed deep in her mind. The rain became even more warm and a bit more oily. The dreamscape became flooded with a red lit dungeon space. She and Armand had been transported there.

"Allow me to cut in," The new voice said. Detective Tau felt overwhelmed. She saw the naked feet of another man. He was a much larger, muscular man. He Ka radiated with a seductive power. She could feel him in her mind, his presence was commanding. Ravina wanted to obey. "I've been looking for you Detective. I have something to show you as well." He leaned forward a bit, and lifted her from beneath her. This brought Detective Tau's head to the perfect position for him to feed himself into her awaiting mouth. He slid closer to Armand, feeding himself- gulp and slight gulp- until Ravina filled by both men. The new man[DOCTOR] seemed to changed the rain's rhythm. He grabbed the back of Armand's head in an embrace, place his other hand over Armand and began leading him in a dance. Each step by the men moved their lengths in, out and around inside of Ravina. She reached up and grabbed his sculpted buttocks. She could taste him. More importantly she could see his intentions. Both her and Armand were shown the same things. There was an Empirical sized planned brewing and the people here in Onyxsia were just the beginning. The Doctor whispered to Armand. Even in their head, Ravina couldn't make out what he was saying. She just sense it was powerful. She felt Armand's rigid length, begin pulsating and beating. He moaned as the sets of their waltz quickened. His release was strong. She could sense his fear and be found repulsion but the Doctor held him in place, continuing their dance. Soon after a few steps, Ravina felt a bolt of lightning in her mind, out side of her in the physical and deep in her loins and *Ka-ra*. Her body shook and a warm river shot from her. The Doctor, pushed Armand out on her mind and body, grabbed her by the neck and released a thunderous venom into her mouth and throat. She felt a click in her mind and suddenly she was lying naked on top of Armand on the roof. They both stirred, looked around and held each other. Neither had words nor thought about what they had just experienced. Armand stood, lifting her, and led them to the seating area beneath the canopy. He pulled her to him tightly as they both hummed the music from the rain.

The Changing Rain

(3 days before the Storms)

Hari Baza crouched in the darkness and scanned the area around him. Although he was the Senior Enlisted Startrooper, this was his first mission to the surface of the planet. The simulators were one thing but being on planet, actually experiencing the effects on the actual fauna and the environment was something no training could prepare you for. Many of the veteran troopers had told them it would be similar to trying to move through mushy gravity for a few hours.

"A muddy dream." Star Trooper First Class Bre'Asha Mix, his training chief said. "You're going to feel like you have a sickness. You should be fine as long as you don't…" he couldn't remember what to he wasn't supposed to do. He did remember that the feeling wouldn't last for a long period of time and he hoped he would remember what she told him. They told him it would be best to use the time to go through the systems checks and get his team locked in. However, none of his cybernetic enhancements and upgrades were fully operational. Training had told him to set the beacon so that the team would have a rallying signal. He would wait for the other two troopers to rally on him and then they could continue their mission until they were extracted. "Wait out the muddy dream," he whispered inside of his helmet. Their mission was reconnaissance and intelligence gathering. But he lost communication with the ship. He was separated from the other troopers. The equipment wasn't working and after laying in the mud on this planet he felt he was losing his mind. The biological parts of him seemed more-alive. Simulators didn't prepare him for what he actually felt and how his organic body would behave. He felt the wind blowing across his body. He could smell the thick dampness of the forest. His brain processed that dampness along with the impending rain. He knew the rain was coming because that was apart of their mission. But now here on the surface there was a damp aroma that spoke to his instincts. "This is how rain smells… " he thought.

Their mission was to observe the surface populace's behavior after the rain's saturation. Hari stood and scanned the forest. He knew he had to find his craft, gear and the other troopers before establishing an observation post.   He could worry about acclimating to the surface conditions once that was done. Spinning slowly he found a small patch of fallen trees and over grown vegetation that would give him shelter. He moved to that patch of bushy growth and began making his small base camp.

(One day before the storm. Two days after crash landing)
Letha leaned against the side of the camouflaged watch tower and listened to the transmissions of the different radio stations. All were discussing the impending storm that would be rolling into the Valley. Onyxsia was nicknamed Storm City due to the amount of storms that ravaged the area. The Corporate ran stations were saying the regular things. Speaking to barometric pressure, possible flooding, in the city's low zones, possible power outages and a disruption in some communications. Citizens were urged to switch to back up battery powered generators tomorrow and stock up essential supplies. This was nothing special. Nothing out of the ordinary. It was the pirate stations that worried her. Sister Shaw spoke about rumors of conspiracies.
"The Corporations are planning something big that may affect our food, drinking water and possibly our lives directly." Her voice had an ethereal feel and was soothing, even over the pirated airwaves. "The Sisterhood

has taken precautions and worked with the various networks to do what we can to help." She spoke about the evacuation plans and which of the Resistance Groups would be responsible for which zones. This is what worried Letha. She and Occa, her sister-wife, were in this part of the Valley, recovering plants, mushrooms and various gems and minerals from their foraging harvests. An influx of people would make their harvesting difficult and a bit more dangerous. She watched Occa sleeping quietly in their hammock and did her best to avoid the pessimistic voice that was whispering in the back of her brain. Occa was the warrior adventurer of the duo. She knew she would be safe during their split while Occa did the deep foraging and recovery of the mushrooms they needed but Letha couldn't help but worry. The dreams scared her. She had visions of a beautiful apartment in the city, suddenly over ran with bugs. The weird and disgusting part was the bugs crawled all over her body; millions of tiny legs tweaking and touching nerve endings. Only instead of being horrified, she was aroused. This sexual arousal scared her even more. In the dream she watched her and Occa covered in bugs but it felt as if she were being gently sexually electrocuted. She was pulled roughly from her sleep as a powerful and prickly orgasm rushed through her. She sat up in the bed, heart pounding. Letha sat on the side of the bed for a few minutes then made tea from some of the herbs.

That was an hour or so ago. A solid hour before dawn. She wouldn't dare wake Occa with talks her dreams. She needed her rest. Where Occa was a warrior, Letha was more witch. She spoke in dreams and spirits. Along with that she could speak to machines. Occa would tease her about how being able to speak to all of the spirits and ghost would drive her into madness. So now she just listen to the radio and monitored the sounds of the Valley. There was no need to worry her.

(Day Two of the storm. Five days after crash landing)

Occa sat beneath the giant palm leaves, chewing mushroom stems and being hypnotized by the sounds of the rain allowing the medicinal mushrooms to began to take effect. The rain had turned into a storm early yesterday evening. She had done a radio check with Letha two hours ago reassured her, that she was safe. Which wasn't a total lie. She had done well to avoid the invasion of people for the city. They were easy to avoid. The women had found an abandoned railroad tunnels that they were able to hide and secure so their stash could be secured. Occa had used it to avoid the people but had gotten cut off by a wahzee (a sudden river formed by a flash flood) so she had to perch in a clump of high bushes and palm trees. So she was safe from the people. What she felt concerned about was the sickness is her body that was growing. The rain was doing something to her and she knew she was going to need to be careful. She hated lying to Letha but there was no need to worry her. Occa had eaten a few grubs to maintain her protein. She would need protein to help with the mushrooms effects. She was in pain. And that pain was growing in intensity and location. She wanted to stay in the caves but being cut off made that an impossibility. So she found a make shift burrow and decided to sit in place. Her body and begun cramping and spasming and she felt this place would be the best and safest to recover(*change*). The pain made her want to sleep. The was a wispy version of her voice in the back of her head told her to eat. So she had been eating as gorging. To help-"with what?"- she asked her and the voice instinctively answered to changed. She before she found this hideaway she ate living proteins and plants. One of the grubs had a vibrant orange and green color. She knew something was off with its appearance but it called to her. She grabbed it, tossed it in her mouth and began chewing. She swallowed as knew immediately that its was wrong. It wasn't poisonous but there was a taste of medicine and crude oil flavor. She quickly foraging for fruit in the Valley. That was a day ago. She had been lying to Letha since then. She knew if she told Letha that she had felt drawn to eat bugs and one of those bugs was poisonous, she would not only worry but would yell and nag; neither of which would be beneficial. She laughed at the thought of Letha pushing through the Valley's jungle to get to her just to spank her. So Occa placed her call beacon in a large tree near her position. She had taken a few opportunities to evacuate her bowels (*you'll need space to grow*-the wispy raspy voice said). Then cleaned herself in the downpour of the rain the dressed again. She crawled back in the the burrow, did her final radio check with Letha, reminding her she would shut her radio off for security, ate another mushroom and began using the large palm leave to cocoon herself.

Hari had began patrolling the area near the fallen craft. At first he wanted to recover as much of the debris as possible. Then he hope he could find signs of the other two cadets. And by the five or so day he patrolled the area to simply fight off complacency. The atmosphere was having less effect on him even though he still felt as if he was still moving through a muddy dream, at least now he was moving faster. The storm had began a few cycles ago and he used the sounds of the down pour to avoid to populants that came from the city. He even saw one- a female, moving stealthily through the jungle and decided to watch her from a safe distance. It was easy to access that she was skilled and well trained. He watched and studied her on different occasions. The first few times he saw her were not special. It wasn't until he watched her undress in the rain and bath herself did he become drawn and attracted to her. It wasn't his first time seeing a female naked. The showers on the ships were uni-gender. The only difference was females had breast and a vagina and male had a penis. Here on the surface, in the rain it was different. As he watched her clean herself, he hungered for her flesh. Her breast hung full and heavy. Her skin tones was a deep dark beautiful brown tone. Her legs were long and powerful. She couldn't take is eyes away from her pubic area. The hair there was thick and plush. Hari thought about burying his face there as sucking her. By the third time he saw her bath in the rain he could actually smell her excited scent. He watched her urinate then waited for her to leave and collect the small patch of leaves. He sucked on the leaves at night and thought of her. Watching her made his penis grow extremely hard. He thought of her as he washed his body. His penis was usually flaccid, except for the occasional girth when he has to urinate badly. Now it was different. It was filled completely. The very head of its modest length turned ,noticeably crooked, to the left like a hook. He took cues from her and ate some of the things she did. He saw a few of the orange grubs that seemed out of place. He *knew* (was programmed) to avoid them. But the jungle roots and fruit he ate along with the packaged food on the ship. Hari lay in his bunk one night completely naked. Thinking of the female ranger. He was half dreaming. One of the items he saw her eat and mimicked made his head swim and his body feel "alive". All of his senses were altered "***upgraded***". Things felt more vibrant and flavorful. And his penis stood stone like erect beneath his blanket. Each movement sent bio electro surges through him. Hari wrapped his hands around his penis. This dreamy awareness made him feel free. He felt a deep hidden urging for his to move his faces on his length. Hari decided to spit large globs of saliva into his palms then glided his his up and down. His thumb rubbed his bent head sending jubilant sparks throughout his body and head. He felt giddy as each stroke moved him further into a euphoric awakening disbelief. He felt bugs playfully crawling beneath his skin. He picture the female ranger smiling and watching him. She was standing over him in his mind rubbing her large breast. Sweet milk dripped from her nipples into his mouth. Hari drank the clear dream juice and pulled on his girth. He was possessed with the urging of a euphoric commanding to be free and release. To feed and be fed. His hands pulled and twisted. A growing warmth ball also grew in his stomach and down inside of his rear hole. He held his eyes closed and internally fixated on the female in his dream mind. As she released her breast, she let one fall into his mouth and laughed. She moved her beautifully glowing hand down to his throbbing penis. She tapped the head with her thumb then wrapped her hand around his length and squeezed. Hari exploded into warm liquid and colors. He screamed and howled in both his dream mind and into the rain of the valley. He was pulled out of him self and watched his naked body convulsing. A thick hot white mucus shot from him in long cords. Hari had never seen or experienced anything like it. He was confused and perplexed. His last memory of the dream was him tasting the mucus then ascending into the space of colors, sounds, vibrations, aromas, songs of his being.

Hari didn't know how long he was out. He didn't bother to check his log data. He was extremely hungry and thirsty. The rain had dissipated some but it didn't stop. The first thing -person - he thought about was the female. After his dream he felt connected to her. He dressed and moved to his patrol. After a few minutes he sat and conducted a listening halt. He took a deep breath and opened his senses to the world. The dream mushroom and the *release* changed him. Hari felt connect to the world in a different way. He felt things differently. He understood everything differently. The rain had a more pronounced taste. As he listened it seemed now everything had a voice. The fauna whispered to him from with in. He was aware of the living energy of the creatures near him. He squinted and focused on what he first thought was distant radio chatter. Then realized it was the rain.

The rain carried a nearly inaudible chatter. He experienced the surfaced for the first time. It excited him. His penis semi erect inside of his pants throbbed in sync with his heart. Hari was finally awake. The sun hadn't rose yet and the damp jungle valley darkness engulfed him but his new awareness made the world seem bright. Hari scanned the immediate and pushed his mind out. Then found what he was looking for- the female ranger. Her *presence* was distinct in the chatter of the atmosphere. She was in pain. He could sense her anguish. Sense her distress. Hari turned off the rest of the sounds in his brain and moved out straight toward the sound of her pain.

Occa lay inside of her makeshift tent and cocoon praying for death to overtake her. Something was disastrously wrong. She had been poisoned by something (*the rain*- something was in the *rain*) and now she felt like she was dying. If she wasn't dying she certainly felt as if she was being tortured. Over the last couple nights, she felt and heard muscles tear and her bones breaking. And the next day or so she was whole again. It moved in cycles like contractions. The raspy voice was more clear. It was calming her. The raspy voice was talking her through the pain.

"This is the *morgi*-the change."

In the dullness of the relief from the painful contractions Occa released she was actually growing. The raspy voice growled a sickeningly in her mind, "You're molting little bug". She felt bigger. She knew had the feeling of being bigger and muscular bloated. She wanted to die. Her head and spine pulsated in a quiet excruciation. She breathed harshly, feeling as if her lungs were being ripped apart. The understanding of the ecdysis process rolled around in her head. Occa screamed from deep with in herself as the knowledge of what was happening sunk in. She used the last bit of awareness and strength to take three of the last mushrooms she had in hopes of ending herself in a deep euphoric slumber.

Hari moved stealthily but purposefully through the jungle. Since his dream things he had been told or information that had been downloaded into his brain and cybernetic intelligence slowly came back to him. He remembered what Star Trooper First Class Mix had said. "You'll be fine as long as you don't eat any of the organic materials that are being delivered. The vegetation and wild life is basically safe to consume.

Somethings may make you ill or intoxicated but your ship's medical download should clear those things up. Just have your team be aware and don't stay out in the rain longer than you have to or consume too of the natural food on the surface."

Hari accessed the top secret documents from the mission scientists.

"Avoid ingesting any organic or biological material the was orange in color. One of which was an alien larvae that was cybernetically enhanced with nanotechnology to force a metamorphosis within humans to change their brain matter and possibly physical make up for the purposes of experimental research."

The information flooded Hari's brain. It became part of his focus and motivation. He had a deep concern for the female ranger. He knew she would probably need help. Especially with the howling and growling of wild animals he had heard in his sleep. Beasts in such anguish must be vicious and dangerous.

Occa felt the waves of pain change. It felt like the were millions of small bites, then tearing and ripping then more small bites. Throughout the night she tossed and turned; rolling back and forth. She felt two large rocks fall beneath her. She listened to the sound of her body be torn and pulled apart. She felt her breast growing inside the her clothing. Occa laughed as another wave of pain rolled through and switched her mind into unconsciousness.

A'Letha Evelynne of the Evelynne Gray Order of Witches, lay naked in front of their cabin. She create a small sacred soil bed to ensure the ritual was done properly. The rain beat on her body in a jagged staccato rhythm. Her eyes were closed and she chanted the words she was taught by the Evelynne Mothers in her coven. She needed to leave her body and find Occa. Occa would tease her about being a witch. About being able to communicate with machines and nature. Letha never told Occa that she used the energy and fluids from their sex to communicate with her spirit and bond them to each other. What she told Occa, was that the copper bracelets connected them on a deeper level.

"It's good luck, my heart," Letha once whispered to her from between Occa's thighs. She rolled her tongue over Occa's clitoris and lips and mumbled a chant. The same chant that she mumbled now, laying naked in the rain. The Connection and Bonding chant. Letha lick and drank Occa's juices and fluid. Embedded in the chant was a secret prayer and trance induction spell. The spell, said during sex as she held Occa fluid in her mouth connected them in the Three Blessed Bodies; Mind, Spirit and Whole. During the first time she used her tongue on Occa and her finger on herself. She opened the gates as they climaxed together. So anytime Letha needed to truly communicate with Occa she just had to ground her self in a bed on sacred soil, say the sacred chant, and have a sexual release. Without Occa here the only way she could do it was to pleasure her self. So laying in rain slowly and purposefully rubbing the warmth of her sex center she mumbled the chant, opened her mind to find Occa. Letha wiggled her body further into the mud. She used the roots of the trees and plants to connect with wires in the ground and moved from different paths ways, both electric and machine to natural. She yelled in her spiritual voice out to Occa. There was a dull soft heart beat from nature and technology. There was something diabolical about the rain's conductivity. Then suddenly she heard Occa call out in a raw passionate pain. It came as a flame orange aura in an audio shriek that was both Occa and not her. She felt larger and more -plump. Her passion was raw, distorted and rousingly grotesque.

Her aroma was sweet and seductive. Letha sensed Occa embracing herself in a (*double arm*), leaving her confused.

Letha continued trying to understand what was going on. While she was spiritually connecting with Occa's aura, Letha's physical form was engrossed in a rough self pleasure. Her body trembled and shook from the orgasms. She pulled back to her own self. She came to, lying on her side. The rain was still falling down. Letha sat up looking around and turned her head toward Occa's energy. She would get dressed and go to find her lover.

Occa woke laying on her side and immediately knew there was something different about her. The rain out of the cocoon she built was subsiding but hadn't stopped. Her body ached and she felt woozy and disoriented as if waking from a drunken stupor. She felt bloated. Yet she had a get hungry growing in her. Her body trembled and tingled. In between her legs felt and smelled like she had multiple orgasms in her sleep. Letha would wake her up licking and kissing her there and there would also be a small puddle of thin creaminess and wonderful sounds of Letha slurping and mumbling to herself. Now Occa lay in a larger thicker stickier mess and was both extremely aroused and hungry. She sat and placed her hands on both sides of her to steady her body.

"*Why do i feel heavier*?" she thought to herself. She looked down at her breast and realized they were swollen. Much more than they were during lunar days. Her nipples throbbed and pulsated. Reached up and to hold them for examination and felt a deep soreness in her back and ribs. She lifted her breast to ease the discomfort of the new weight of them. A new instinct of inspecting them further came over her. Occa watched as four hands rolled and lifted her breast. The her brain registered want her eyes saw. She had much larger breast and four hands. Horrifying shock ran through Occa as she slowly raised the four hands as arms up so that she could see them as clearly as she could in the light of the cocoon. She shrieked and stood to her new fully height and ran screaming from the hidden spot she had cocooned her self. She pushed through the jungle's vegetation blinded by the ran and fear, and collided head first into a solid mass and fell unconscious.

Hari had patrolled the area near where he had saw the female ranger for two night with no visual signs of her. The jungle near where she had been was now thick with the presence of different species of insects. There was also a heavy and powerful aroma, even with his helmet and filter, that made her extremely aroused and frantic for her. The vegetation was thicker that in had been, as well. It sounded as if he had strayed near the lair of a large beast but he couldn't be sure. On the third day her discovered a beacon's signal different from his and he decided to go there and investigate. When he arrived near the area he sat among the larger plants as waited in the shadows. Being on the surface was very new for him. He took this time to observe the jungle activity. He saw people in small groups move in small frantic caravans past him. He over heard a few people mumbling about bugs and the rain. It had began to slowly in a normal downpour. He thought his mission-he hadn't thought about the other two cadets since their launch. He now knew that the purpose of their mission was to observe the populace and how they were affected by the rain. That knowledge wasnt just due to his training; his instincts and exposure to the storms informed him. The rain had changed him as well.

A movement to his immediate left, with in 100 meters of where he sat, caught his attention. He turned slowly and saw what he believed to be a woman with translucent gray eyes staring back at him. For a second he thought it was a reflection from the wet leaves but she moved and stared directly at him.

"Why was she here," he wondered. He blinked and lost track of her. His helmet's sensors were no help because of the storm and his inexperience with being on the surface. He kept his weapon ready and changed his position to that he could observe where the woman had been as well as the area where the ranger's beacon had been. Just as Hari was moving deeper into a deeper position into the bush and grunting noise and a feral scream broke the silence. Hari turned and took two steps toward the sound and was tackled by the fleeing female danger who had been hiding in the darkness. He heard her head collide with the armor plating on his shoulder pad. The force knocked him into a tree and sent him to the ground. Disoriented Hari slowly began gathering himself and moving to stand up when the gray eyes woman dove at him from the shadows. He watched in slow motion as she was swinging two large knives and him at different angles.

"Get away from her!"

The blades slammed into his suit and her forced knocked them both to the ground.

Letha used her connection to Occa to get her close to where she knew she would be. She also had the small receiver that also picked up the beacon's encrypted pulse. She had been moving stealthy through the jungle and only needed a day and a half of hiking to reach the area where she "felt" Occa to be. She knew she was close. Not only did the homing beacon receiver show her that, her body buzzed and tweaked as he got closer. Her heart rate pick up as well. Her nipples were erect beneath her rain poncho and wet shirt and her sex center buzzed. The sweaty lubricant during the walked caused her to stop a few times to have powerful orgasms and sleep. Now as got closer she was filled and nerves and arousal. Even the damp jungle air smelled of Occa's sex. The faint scent of her pheromones was in the air. Letha kneeled to catch her breath and adjust her pack. Occa was close. Just as she began to stand to caught a glimpse of a man in a Star Trooper battle suit. She froze. She had forgotten about the crash landing that happened a few days ago. Heart pounding and arousal and fear pumped through her blood. She tried scanning the jungle looking for others. Usually the Star Troopers travel in pairs or three person team. She touched the ground and attempted to scan his suit. She discovered that his suit was not linked to the mother ship but she realized the trooper was also tracking Occa's beacon signal. Her glowing gray eyes pierced through the visor and further into his suit. Letha knew she was have to kill him to protect Occa. She felt him Hunting Occa. He was filled with deep lustful passion-hunger. He was salivating over the thought of Occa. Letha caused his suit to flutter and twitch allowing her to disappear. She dropped to the ground again. That's when the full understanding of Occa was communicated to Letha. Occa was sick and hiding just 50 meters from the Trooper's position. She removed her pack and pulled her blades free and rolled over on her feet. The trooper instinctively moved himself so that he could face Letha and still keep eyes on Occa. Letha began crawling toward the trooper blades drawn. And without warning Occa screamed and came running from her hiding place. Letha froze. Not from fear or indecision. It was Occa. She was taller by 6 inches. Her breasts were pulled free of her torn uniform top. She was bigger. Thicker, *longer* and more voluptuous and curvaceous. And she had FOUR ARMS! Letha gasped as she watched Occa slam into the trooper, knocking him over. Letha watched Occa fall backward. That's when she sprung into action. She swung the

blades in the precise places to not only disable the battle suit , but also cause a small short circuit. The effect would nearly cook him from the inside. Before he could respond, Letha was atop of him, smashing the blades into his body and screaming. "GET AWAY FROM HER!"
She swung and pounded on his ecso-suit. He held his arms up over his face to shield himself from the blows. Letha ripped and tore at him with ferocity. The trooper grunted and kicked up at him sending her off of him.

Hari had been caught off guard. The Ranger had knocked him over and before he could truly react the woman in the shadows was attacking him. This attacked wasn't like the training fights. Her use of the blades was overwhelming. He tried his best to defend against her movement but he seemed an instant to slow or an ounce to weak. The suits emergency settings were going off. The internal temperature was rising quickly. That's when the understanding of what the woman was doing shocked Hari. Her strikes were shutting down the suits brain as if she were attacking the cybernetic nervous system. The suit normal functions are being over-ridden and it's acting like the human body.All of the systems are acting as if it's losing limbs. The only recourse is for the suit to save the vital organs causing the circuitry to overheat. If he doesn't eject soon he will be cooked inside of the exso suit. The immense drowsy arousal was replaced to a shot of adrenaline. Hari covered his head to defend against her blades and then kicked her off of him. Once she was off him, he quickly used the emergency sequence to disengage the suit from him. The armor fell in small chunks of pieces around him. He wrestled he under layer from his body frantically, as the electro veins and connections sparked and zapped him. He pulled the top and bottom free, not realizing he was standing naked in front of both of women. He held his hands up to show he was as not trying to fight. Both women were staring at him. The woman with her blades, was on his left and the Ranger was on his right. And without warning the Ranger, omitted a sound that was part high pitched moan and a guttural hiss. Then the space around them was overcome with a thick flowery misty aroma. Then a feeling on of dreaming in slow motion overcame him. He watched in slow motion as the ranger grabbed the woman by the throat with her upper right hand. Hari heard her whisper in his head to the woman [*Letha:my wife:LOVER!*] "undress… I want to taste you".

As the woman (Letha) began undressing the ranger [*Ma'Occa:Queen:lover*] grabbed him by the throat with her upper left hand and lifted him from him feet. She used her lower left hand and slowly began stroking his dangling meat. She lifted the woman the air and used her lower right hand to gently insert inside of the woman. Hari tossed his left hand out and touched the free hand of Letha, who instinctively held it. A warm lusting fear rolled through Hari as he felt a neurological connection click in his brain and he was synced to the two women. Occa was both shocked and amazed at what she was experiencing. She felt a new deeper connection to Letha and they both were linked to the man[*Hari: soldier:lover].* She felt a deep and ravenous sexual connection and hunger from him. They all were covered in her new scent. His thickness throbbed in her hand. She craved the sweet taste of Letha, who smelled sweet and earthy. Occa worked her fingers in and out until they were coating her hands. She lifted Letha slightly higher, until her crotch was at Occa's mouth. She guided Hari to the ground and pulled him between her thighs. She felt his tongue began working. The three of them trembled and shuddered in an orgasmic state or bliss.

Letha felt her connection to Occa change once she had began attacking the trooper. It wasn't until she smelled Occa's new aroma and felt the actual mist engulf the area did she understand something was different. Letha knew the rain was the cause of the (*morgi*) change. She relived all the moments after Occa had consumed the orange bug. The pain. The lustful connection with the trooper[Hari:soldier:lover/mate]. She sensed the gentle comfort Occa felt when she knew Letha was on the way. And the violent pleasure sensing them fighting. When she felt the   trooper reaching out, it was on multiple levels. Letha took his hand hers and was swarmed with a complete submersion of knowledge. She understood the pride of his training. She knew the terror and shame he felt when the ship crashed and he lost his crew. She knew about the plan and the diabolical truth about the watch. She felt his hunger for Occa and his need to protect her. She felt his long hot organic muscle throbbing and sending signals out. This organic and biological arousal was new to him. It was engineered out of him. But now he was new and begging to he reprogrammed. Letha desired to be imprinted on him and have him be imprinted on her and Occa. A hunger rose in her. Then she felt Occa's thick saliva covered tongue and mouth cover her sex portal. She gasped him pleasure and Occa's tongue rolled between her little witchy lips. Letha shudder and she felt the sensation of the trooper's tongue and mouth drink and slurp at Occa's creamy place. Letha allowed herself to float in to the passionate stream of pleasure created by the three of them. She didn't notice the multiple orgasmic waves that poured sweet nectar from her and over Occa's face and engorged breasts. She only felt the warmth of the new neuroconnection she shared with them.

Occa continued drinking and feeding on Letha until she felt her body go limp. She eased her to the ground next them then pushed Hari backward. Occa crawled atop of him; feeling powerful. She used her upper hands to grip his neck. The feeling of squeezing him made her want him more. She used one of her lower arms to feed him into her steamy warmth. She eased completely down on him and growled gleefully into the thick jungle air. She placed her lower hands on his wrist and worked her pelvis into his. She hadn't had the pleasure of a man inside of her in a long time. It felt as if both she and Hari were new and this. Rediscovering pleasure. Her new body shudder and shook with a primal pleasure. Her breast flopped and swayed beneath her until she felt Hari take one in his mouth. She felt like a QUEEN/Mother/slut as his greed hunger and new discover of pleasure cheered and urged her movements. Letha moved close to her and gripped her free breast with one arm and pulled herself deeper and closer with the other. A deep sense of wanting to be connected ran through them all. Letha transmitted a powerful de ja vu sense of a dream to them all. A new feeling of bugs crawling all over and into them. The sickening sexual feeling swallowed them all. Neither of them noticed the rain and began falling harder, Splashing and crackling against their skin. They could only think about the others and themselves as new colony.

Occa moved her hands from her throat and placed them on his chest, still holding him by the wrist. Letha moved quickly to sit on his face and pulled Occa's breast into her mouth- alternating one then the other. Letha made a soft "popping" noise as a sweet milky secretion leaked from Occa's nipples. A squishy-squashy sound came from between Occa's legs.

Occa adjusted her long powerful legs, moved her feet beside Hari's thighs and began bouncing on his throbbing length. She felt a swarm of the *bugs* swirling in her stomach. The release she craved had never been this powerful. She bounced moaned and growled in pleasure. She was both energized and exhausted. Letha sucked and massaged Occa's breast, the milk that was just leaking before was running slightly now and covering them all. Occa closed her eyes and thought- I'm going to exploded-loudly into their three minds. Just as a muffled voice replied, "SO!AM!I!" Occa released another much larger and louder sweet-aromatic misting over them all. She bounced a few more times then moved just as Hari's meat exploded between her and Letha. Coating their breasts with his seed. Letha stroked with her hands, then quickly, pushed forward and crawled atop of his thickness. She rolled her hips and eased him in and continued rolling her hips and pelvis over his still throbbing length. She licked at the mixture of his pleasure sauce and Occa's sweet milk. She pulled Occa's face to hers and kissed her. Hari gripped her hips and arched his back, sending him upward and deeper into her. Occa gathered herself and stood over Letha. She caressed the sides of Letha's head with her lower arms, she held her newly larger breast against herself and pinched her nipples. Occa surprised herself as the milkiness ran from her breast. She lost herself in the dual pleasures of Letha's tongue between her legs and the immense tingling sensation beneath her skin. She listened internally as her connection with Hari, transmitted his confused wonderment and bliss. In his thoughts, Occa realized this all was new to him. These sensations and emotions. This new sense of organic bliss. "Emotional deprivation and numbness was how *THEY* controlled the troopers. She felt their connection deepen. She knew at that moment Letha felt it too. She could hear her mumbling the say things as she had with her. She knew now is was a bonding ritual. He would be thiers fo ever. They were all tribe,hive,team. A pink, purple, blue-ish cloudy explosion of pleasure erupted from between her thighs she trembled violently as Letha gripped her butt cheeks. Occa felt like her bladder was emptying as hot fluid ran down her thighs covering Letha as Hari. She held onto to Letha, who was panting and moaning. Hari was also grunting and moaning loudly. He exploded first. A warm white flash move from him through the two women. Letha pulled Occa closer, holding her tightly around her thighs as she shook and panted. The light she omitted was vibrant smoky wave that filled their heads. Occa collapsed backward onto her butt. Letha slumped forward and laid atop of Occa. Their hearts beat is a harmony of

rhythms and tempos. The three of them lay naked and spent and the rain continued.
it was Hari's mind that alerted them first.
"This isn't safe. We are exposed."
With the neurosync still strong the three of them knew to gather their items and move back to the burrow Occa had created to shelter herself. They all crawled inside and waited out the last bit of the storm.

Glossary

Afro-Techo Shaman-An Afro-Techno Shaman is a hypothetical concept that merges elements of African spirituality, technology, and the shamanic tradition. This theoretical figure possesses unique powers that combine the ancient wisdom of traditional shamanism with the advancements and possibilities offered by modern technology.

B.I.R.D.-The Brain Integration Reality Development Stations

Caenite- Race of Witches.

Chasa. is an animal that would be close to a Bison. Its hide is processed to have a raw velvet texture. Material of the common nomad.

C.O.C.K. (Cybernetic.Organic.Copulation.Konnector) -a cybernetic penis enhancement.

Complex biotechno-linguistics: refers to the interdisciplinary field that investigates the intricate interaction between biology, technology, and language. It explores the complex relationship between living organisms, advanced technology, and linguistic systems, focusing on the study and decoding of the language embedded in biological systems and the technological tools used to manipulate them. This includes deciphering the genetic code, analyzing the language of DNA and RNA sequences, and understanding the linguistic patterns that govern biological processes.

Dah-di(as in My Dah-di) a term of endearment used by an alien being who is in sexual or otherwise intimate subservience to a man.

Eblast bullets- An EMP type round that disrupts and shuts down smaller targets such as robots, bio mechanical, cybernetic and androids on a localized level.

Electric Field Sensors: sensors that act as an early detection devices for hidden electrical harvesting fields. The sensors omit a signal that can be detected by security systems.

Evelynne- Gray Order of Witches Initially, the coven's power blossomed through a deep connection with nature. They harnessed the energies of earth, wind, and water, communicating with flora and fauna. The Evelynne Order's rituals involved intricate dances, chants, and the use of herbal potions to heal the sick and protect their communities.

Gharvelian- a Harpy humanoid alien race.

Ka-Total life force minus the physical state. It consists of a person's aura(ka-ra)their spiritual vibrations and sounds(ka-bu), spiritual scents (ka-su),spiritual taste (ka-ci), and spiritual awareness (ka-mi). Kamala are a mystical sect people who study and pattern their life on the understanding of Ka. Most Kamala can understand and interpret parts of the Ka. While more devote practitioners can enter into the spiritual realm and actually work with Ka-Pur.

Kasha- is a fabric similar to a satin cotton blend. Used for delicates such as underwear, sheets and lingerie type items.

Knight's Movement-The time jump is what is known as a Knight's Movement Theory or Knight's Jump. Named so because it allows the jumper to go back in time three jumps and over one reality or over three realities and one time jump.

Length- is a measure of a person's height. It isn't an approximate measurement. It is roughly 1 and a quarter feet.

LINEAGE-Cyborg Convent of Nuns who think the Old Testament is a book of Magic spells and War Tactics. Their devotees are groomed in *"Adonitology"*

longa flower-carnivorous plant that consumes bugs and small animals/birds. It has a sweet intoxicating serum that can be used as a hallucinogenic or to create a wine like beverage.

Lumlum(man, woman, people)-It is a religious sect. The LumLum people are spiritual herbalist. Their witch craft is based on nature's law. Similar to what we would consider witch doctors.

Lunar Prime Rythmn-The Circadian rhythm for the Prime Moon and Planet Arreit. The Divine Rhythm is the basis and source of Techno Shaman Ahlem Rhodes' power and cosmic spiritual connection

M.A.L.I.K. Units- Mechanized Assassin Life-form Killers. A cyborg unit of former soldiers used to hunt down enemies of the Lineage mangoon fruit-On Earth it would a grape the size of a cantaloupe

Morgi-the process similar to the ecdysis process for bugs.

NaVollan.-A humanoid like race from the Planet Calah.

P.U.P. (Personal Uplink accompanying Protection) Drone.

SincoLabs- A Galactic Corporation That focused biotechnology research and development.

Symbiotic Kinetically-charged, Integrated Nanotechnology suit, commonly known as S.K.I.N.

Taurian-Race of Amazonian people. The Taurian people are a Matriarchal Society.

Udugu/Sisterhood: A group of women connected on a spiritual level. They lead a counter establishment group.

Wahzee- a sudden river formed by a flash flood

Tyzine Corporation: a MegaGalatic Empirical Corporation.